why no
goodbye?

Also by the author

Monster Maria / Marisol y El Huracán María

Ronit & Jamil

Homer the Little Stray Cat

New Beginnings

The Bonsai Curator

Plagiarist

Visitation Rites

why no goodbye?

pamela l. laskin

Leapfrog Press
Fredonia, New York

Published in 2019 in the United States by
Leapfrog Press LLC
PO Box 505
Fredonia, NY 14063
www.leapfrogpress.com

Printed in the United States of America

Distributed in the United States by
Consortium Book Sales and Distribution
St. Paul, Minnesota 55114
www.cbsd.com

Proceeds from the sale of this book will be donated to
Fortify Rights

First Edition

Library of Congress Cataloging-in-Publication Data

Names: Laskin, Pamela L., author.
Title: Why no goodbye : why no bhine / Pamela Laskin.
Description: First edition. | Fredonia, NY : Leapfrog Press LLC ; St.
Paul,   Minnesota : Distributed in the United States by Consortium
Book Sales and Distribution, 2019. | Summary: When his mother es-
capes Myanmar with his siblings during the Rohingya crisis, thirteen-
year-old Jubair expresses anger over the abandonment and struggles to
find forgiveness, in a series of letters.
Identifiers: LCCN 2019021546 | ISBN 9781948585064 (pbk. : alk.
paper)
Subjects: LCSH: Rohingya (Burmese people)--Juvenile fiction. |
CYAC: Novels in verse. | Rohingya (Burmese people)--Fiction. |
Abandoned chilldren--Fiction. | Separation (Psychology)--Fiction. |
Refugees--Fiction. | Letters--Fiction. | Burma--Fiction.
Classification: LCC PZ7.5.L37 Wh 2019 | DDC [Fic]--dc23
LC record available at https://lccn.loc.gov/2019021546

To the Rohingya Muslims of Myanmar

Acknowledgements

The cover photo is of Rafiqul, a boy from Myanmar. He has been living with his father in a refugee camp in Bangladesh since September 2017, and is waiting for his mother to join them. The photo was taken by the riverside in Shaporir Dip, Bangladesh, a popular place for refugees to cross from neighboring Myanmar. Rafiqul is currently studying in high school grade 8, and would like to continue his education in the future.

Photograph © 2018 Lewis Inman, lewisinman.com.

Special thanks to Matthew and Amy Smith, Fortify Rights.

Thank you RF CUNY, Grant cycle 49, for financial support of the book.

And to my agent, Myrsini Stephanides, Carol Mann Agency, and finally to Samantha Reiser, who consistently fights for human rights all over the world!

Escape to Malaysia
New York Times, June 6th, 2015

How could you leave
your first born,
how could you tell him
his father is dead,
when you are crossing the sea
to Malaysia
with the babies
where he might be.

True
it was full fare
to pay the smugglers
to take Jubair, too,

but you never
even told him
or even
said good-bye.

Part I: Letters to *May-may**

*Mother

Why did you leave, *May-may*?

You know I cannot write,
so why are you writing me?
I gaze at the long, dirt road
which leads to more dirt.
Keh-bah! *

*Help

Why didn't you teach me to read or write?
You know how to.
It was another gift you kept from me!
Where is my *Pay-pay?* *
Did he die on the ferry
on the boat
in the air?

*Father

Something terrible happened.
I can still hear your screams
and men
with mean smiles
on their faces,
guns that were arms
arms that were guns
thought nothing
of firing their rage
wildly in our village
and *May-may*
children
were never spared.

You never taught me to read or write.
Ha Jia is teaching me. He wants to read me your letters.
You can keep your letters
same way you keep my two brothers and sister with you.
Why didn't you say *bhine?* *

*Goodbye

I may learn how to read and write,
but I still sleep on the soil.
Last night was a monsoon.
Ha Jia let me sleep inside,
"but just one time"
he has told me.
Everyone in *Thayet Oak*
knows me,
so sometimes
there are bamboo houses
where I can sleep
for the night.

Yaq! *
Your letters should stop!

*Stop

One night
they barged into the hut
military men
and you told us
to pretend
to sleep,

but I heard
the shrieking
the crying
saw the pools of red
bleeding on the floor,

"Please stop.
Yaq.*
Stop."

And the men,
they laughed,
and when my sister,
just a baby cried
they laughed
even harder.

*Stop

Ha-Jia says seven is the magical number.
There are five children in his hut.
Hia-Jia and Len-Wen make it seven
and I am the eighth
I am the other child.
What is magic, Mama?
I do not think I have some.
Did you not have enough money
to take me?

I never cursed you before.
I never thought I would.
I would never do this to your face
like street kids do,
but now I am one of them.

Gway Htoot *
to you!

Gway Htoot: Burmese profanity

19

I want to stamp you
in the soil
and stamp my feet
till you are crushed like the snake
I step on.
You will drown in the rain.
You will cough
when the soil is dry,
and my ears
will not moisten you.
Thayet Oak means mango orchard
in our language.

Where are they?
*Qui Ma.**

Qui Ma: Burmese profanity

Where do words come from?
You are like the rat who eats the garbage
leaving us so little food.
Ha-Jia does not understand why I write
I hate you.
I will not read your letters.

Your last words to me?
"Don't cry.
Don't be sad.
Stay well."

Lee Gon *
to you

Lee Gon: Burmese Profanity

Your screams:
Yaq.
Yaq.
Yaq.

Your pleas:
my babies.

Please protect
my babies,

and their laughter
rings in my ears
like a nightmare typhoon
that gets bigger
and uglier
with each monster laugh.

How do you get these letters to me?
Why do you write them?
They are like garbage.
Why did you take my older brother
and leave me tired
and hungry?
How did my father die?

At night, when it is raining
just rain, not storms
I cry for my brother, especially my younger one
I cry for my sister
I cry while the sky
cries with me.

I will write longer letters
when I can do it on my own.
For now I sleep on the soil
and wonder if you feel sad for me
or mad
like I am.
I am like the mandrake in the soil.
I fester
I rot.
And there are ants,
mountains of them
sleeping next to me.

I learned this today.
I can write it, too.
I am a hard worker.
I am an ox.
I am a whale.
This is what Ha-Jia says.
I am dependable.
I like that sound of this:
dependable.
It sounds
like I am someone important.

Why do other Muslims
hate us so?
We are Rohingyas.
We are Muslims, too.
Even the monkeys who roam freely
laugh at me
and they are free.

They laugh like the monsters
who hurt you
and drank blood
for fun.

I had a dream.
I always knew about dreams
even when I could not read
or write.
We are all together
even Papa
who you say
is dead.
My insides do not feel dead
because we are laughing
and Jaynu acts like a clown.
Our little girl,
the princess
she laughs so loud
it makes the sky thunder
in happiness,
and Papa brings back meat
and our stomachs
are full.

Now I know more words,
so I can tell you,
my back is broken from the water pails
I must carry every day
and from the little sleep I get
with a blanket of angry stars above me.
There are dead dogs
in the water,
but Ha Jia
says he boils the water
so I will not get sick.
The air smells
of rot.
I am thirteen soon, I think.
I do not remember my birthday.
Do you?
Do my brothers and sister
remember me?
Why did you take my older brother?

Here is my day:
I wake up tired.
I wake up hungry.
I want to cry.
There is no time for this.
I eat some rice.
I drink some water.
Then I go fetch water
and fetch
and fetch
and fetch
till my arms collapse at my sides
like two dead trunks
of broken wood.

Ha Jia told me you were once beautiful
he told me you dreamed of going to school
of writing poetry.
He said you loved books
and language.
Words were a gift
you kept to yourself
Why didn't you share them, *May-may?*
Were you that greedy?
I like them, too.

Why did you write
to tell me this?
This is the first letter you wrote that I am reading.
I will not read the letters in order
if I read them at all.
But telling me
you are in a refugee camp
and what you ate for breakfast.
I want to strangle the rope from the bucket
around your dirty neck.

Here is what I ate for breakfast today.
Nothing.
There was not enough food
for all the children.
Two kernels of rice
nothing
for a crying stomach,
and the monkeys ran around
with bananas.

We had a hut
it was bamboo
and sometimes it felt moist
since the river was inside,
but it was our hut.

We had a hut
with four children,
sometimes there was laughter
sometimes there was *mohinga* for dinner,
but always
there was a warm body
to feel next to you,
and someone
to share stories with.

We had a hut
a mat to sleep on
we never walked under the clothesline,

we had a hut
and I had a hug
even though I had to share it.

This is what I think
one day I had a father
he farmed, he made some money
sometimes we ate *laphet*
sometimes we could not,
but we were a family.
He left
for safety
for the family,
but he didn't take the family.

This is what I know
that is some cruel joke
since you are gone, too.

You said he died
you do not know how,
but now you are alone.

You are not alone.
You have three other children.
I am alone.
And there are water rats
to keep me company.

You have died for me.

And the nightmares
of the military men
laughing in the wind
keep me scared
every sleeping moment.

Did he really die?
How?
This does not seem real,
nor do the bush fires.
Nor do the bullets I hear all around.
Sometimes, at night, the bullets dance
they weave in and out of stars
like a bad nightmare.

Why didn't he come home
when he knew the men
had hurt you?

You couldn't even rise
from the floor.

This is what I think
(and this is what Ha Jia told me)
we have no citizenship
no jobs
no benefits,
no education
our mosques were destroyed
monuments and cemeteries
destroyed;

this is what I know
Pay-pay was smart to die
(if he really died)

because we have no future.

Why did you name me Jubair?
it is an odd name
an uncomfortable name,
no one else has it.

I want what everyone else has
a normal name
a mat to sleep on
the indoors
a home.

Last night
a monkey shrieked in my face
and I screamed at him
till my voice
was gone;

I saw that his face
was filled with terror.

This is what I think
I used to play
I used to clap
my sister jumped rope,
sometimes I skipped around
with nowhere to go.
I helped with chores,
but I was not the only one.

Once I saw a balloon,
and this is what I know
it was colorful and bright
but it disappeared
in the sky.

This is what I know
the sky at night
is filled with monster sounds-
hissing,
screeching
sometimes girls
plead
no
no
no,

and there are guns
going off
cries
no
no
no,

the monkeys wail
for their Mamas;

yes,
I want to get out of here,
but how?

This is what I think
tomorrow
when I wake up
may be the last day.

This is what I know
If I die
I can meet *Pay-pay*
in the after-life
if there is one.

Ha Jia told me
it was hard for you
across the strait of Malacca
across the Adaman Sea,
especially with the little ones,

that so many of our people
never made it.

This is what I know
it is harder
for me
to sleep with sounds
than silence.

Sometimes
just sometimes
I play with Ha Jia's children.
We play hide and seek.
They work hard, too
they plant
dig their soil
deep into the earth
till their nails
are all dirt,
but they do not carry heavy loads
on their backs,

when I play
I remember
I am just a boy
not a man
carrying a man's worries
heavy on my back.
*Nga Lo Chit Mae Thu.**

*You are driving me crazy!

I like the letter telling me about songs
I read it, *May-may.*
I like that you sing at the camps
songs float in the air
a gentle breeze
that lifts you far away, you say.

Where?
To come back and get me.

Sometimes I will read a letter—or two
if I am not too busy
or tired.

Sometimes the forest is a monster:
the gunfire,
the sound of the tamarinds
the snakes
the hungry rats,

Sometimes it is a song
sweet
dream-like,
teasing me
to run like the wind.

I am reading books, *May-may*.
There are not many here,
but I read whatever Ha-Jia finds.

One day
he went to the capital
and found a whole load
that people threw out
in the garbage.

Some people may say they stink
but I say they smell
of what I can know
if I keep them
close.

Mama writes me, and I decide to read her letter

I never taught you to write
since I never wanted you to dream.
My dreams were once
the sun
the moon
the seas.
I forgot I was a girl.
I forgot I was a Ronhingya.

I never taught you to read
since I did not want you
to discover
there was more than the little
I could give to you-
a world beyond our small place
where people went to work
and their words mattered.

I never taught you to read or write
since I was afraid
for you to try to fly;
I knew there was no fuel in our world
and your wings,
which were enormous
would only come
crashing down.

Don't worry.
I would not dare to dream.
Where could it possibly
take me?

This is what I know
dreams are stupid.

There is a girl
in the woods
I see her peeking out through the leaves.

Her face
is like a leaf
big
beautiful
bright
scared of the light.

Is she a dream?
Ha Jia told me about mirages,
maybe that is all she is
because if I blink my eyes
she is gone.

If she is real
I will take her to the beach.
One time
the whole family took a trip;
we even stayed overnight.
the sand was so white
it was opaque
(I learned this word
from a book I have been reading
The Good Earth
by Pearl S. Buck),

and the sky
the sea
blue
like the blue could burst
through clouds,

beautiful blue
not sad blue.

I could not leave the water
Pay-pay called me merman.

This memory
sits still
and silent
inside,

until I am ready
to give it
to someone
special.

Do you think the author's
real name is Pearl?
Could she
have made it up?
The life in China
was hard
hard like the water buckets
I carry on my back
which scrape my shoulders
ragged,

Pearl
is a fantasy
of being precious,
how can you be poor
and precious?

How can I read this now?
It has only been months
since you left
the season changed from wet to dry,
and now it is dry again
and hot
the heat is a menace
a maniac,
but so can the water be, sometimes.

I will tell you more about the water
in my next letter.

Yes,
I read another letter you wrote
about the weather
how the camps
have ferocious heat, too,
how the burka you wear
is saturated in sweat,
how Amana cries,
since I was her favorite brother.

Do not tell me this.
It opens up my sorrow
and makes it bigger.
I do not need
sorrow to slice
through my skin.

If I were an author
I would name myself
Abracadabra,

so I could make magic
with words
and my words would travel
in the wind
would make Amana's tears
dry off
take flight.

This is what I know
Ha Jia told me
but I read it
in a ripped article
I found in the forest:

many of our people
are stranded
at sea,
Thailand
Indonesia
no one
wants us
the way you
did not want me
and left.

This is what I think
you can't love
anyone afterwards—
can you?

The article
goes on to say
so many migrants died
in overcrowded
and unseaworthy boats,
so I suppose
I am lucky
my family is alive.

The weather
this past summer
it rained
as if that is all
it could do,
it rained unkindly
it rained till I lived with rain
and water;
I could fill my bucket
with tears from the sky
but I was never dry,
since I had so many tears inside me.
Perhaps I always will.

Once
there was a monsoon
July or August
I can't keep track
of the months,
but the rain
was heartless,
not even good for the crops
Ha Jia said,
but he let
me stay inside,
which
I have done
a few times,
but this time
Lia made soup
and the greens floated to the top,
and filled my belly
with happiness.

Pagodas,
precious pagodas
praying pagodas,

but what about
when your prayers
go unanswered
praying mantis,

who attacked me,
so my welt
now rises
like a pagoda
off my bony arm.

Part II: The Girl in the Woods

And on the night
of the biggest monsoon,
the littlest boy, Amana's age,
he cuddled with me
and I could pretend
it was the girl
I have seen
in the forest,

and I could make believe
I was keeping her safe
like Zatoup
felt
with my arms
wrapped around him.

Now it is hot, *May-may*
sometimes there is a breeze,
but mostly it is hot,

even so
I see her eyes peeking out
from behind the bushes,

this is what I know
this is
a good heat.

Hot
blazing hot
mean hot
sweat is another skin hot
hot for her
so hot for her
my body
makes more heat.

This is a letter
I will not send you, *May-may*.

Is it a year
since you left?
I can really
read and write
which makes me
a little less lonely,

but I may not
write you so often anymore
there is a girl
she has come
out of the woods
to stare at me,
she will not say a word,

but my eyes are stuck.

This girl
darts in and out of the leaves
like shade or shadow
she has long, dark hair
and night eyes
with stars in them
white specks;
they are large
and lonely
she wants to see me,
but she can't look
into my eyes.

Shin aaingaliutlo pway lar? *

*Do you speak English?

Hi!
No Answer.
She slips out of the shadows
like a thief.
Shin-ne-meh-beh-lo-k'aw-leh?
What is your name?
I say it in English.
No answer,
but she hovers over me
as I fill the buckets
with water.
I offer her some,
but she will not even
open her mouth.
She doesn't even smile.

May-may
I cannot write you anymore
for some time
I have met a girl.

This is what I know
I want her
to be my friend
or maybe something more.

Can't you talk
can't you
at least smile?

and suddenly
it emerges
a smile
thin as the moon
radiant
white, white, white
against
dark, dark skin
darker than mine
and dirty.

She allows me to wash her face off
with water from the stream.
*Sain bhaalkalell? ***

*Where are you from?

72

Where do you sleep at night?
Do you sleep?
Where do you live?
Do you live in the forest like I do?
Do we speak the same language?
Do you speak at all?
Do you understand me?

Can you answer me?

Kyasopataal. *

*Welcome

*Come over
sit by my side
watch how I pour the water
into the pail,
the grass will tickle
the inside of your long, brown legs,
and I can rub them, too.*

*But you won't let me
near you,
not near enough
to smell your sweet breath
and soothe your sorrow.*

I will need
Kan-kaung-ba-zay *
with her.

*Good luck

74

Dear *Pay-pay*,

I know you are dead,
but there is no way
I am telling this
to my *May-may*.

There is this girl
who sneaks out of the woods
to watch me fill the pails
with water.

She comes to the streams
stands and stares,

but she will not even look at me,
and at night
when stars fill the sky
she sleeps on the same floor as I do—
the woods,
but so far, far away.

Pay-pay,

My body
is on fire,
what do I do with it.

The water
does not cool me off
and she still hasn't said a word.

Come
sleep next to me
you can sleep
on the other end of the mat.

And she does.

Min-ga-la-ba. *

Why is she saying
hello to me
now?

* Hello

In the morning
we are strangers again.

Sometimes
when I am at Ha Jia's house
I play a game
called tag with his children;

this is what
she does with me
darting in and out of the woods.

Or it is peek-a-boo
a game
you played with me
when I was a baby.

Do you remember, *May-may*?
Do you remember me?

I don't even know
how old I am,
but however old it is
she, with the sneaky smile
is the same age.

When I read a letter of yours
like today
when you tell me about
how the boys are learning
to read,

I pretend
the letter
is you,
so I can rip it into tiny shreds
and throw it away.

Dear *May-may*,

At night she sleeps next to me
at the other end
of the mat.
I beckon her closer,
but she barely looks at me
and doesn't touch me,

though when she sleeps
and the night has a breeze
her sleep is the wind
that wills me
to close my eyes.

You can talk to me
I won't bite you.

Where are you from?
*Sain bhaalkalell? **
Why are you here?
Why do you follow me
and when I try to talk to you
run like a rat
who has been trapped
for supper?

You know English
since you understand
what I am saying.

*Where are you from?

And this is why I said rat
I hate women
I am telling you
I hate girls
all girls,
except maybe my sister;
I might hate her, too
I do not know
it's been almost a year and a half
since I have seen her.

Women have left me
their voices are not true
like the earth,

yet when I say this
suddenly, there is a voice.

I am not all women
you tell me;
I am a girl
though I have been treated like a woman
that is why I am here.

Tell me
I reach out my hand,
You can tell me anything.
What is your name?

And then she moves closer
My name is Zahura
I will talk to you
as long as you stop cursing about girls
beneath your breath.

Did I do that?
Really?
Now I will stop
and listen.

She tells me
how she has run away
from her village
very far away.
She is fourteen
and says they will kill her.

She loved school
before they made her stop,
because it is time
for her to earn money for the family.

There is a man
in the village
for whom they can get
get money
and Zahura will have a real home,
(that is what he says)
only the man
is forty-five.

She tells me
even before
the man
there was a boy
her brother's friend
who touched her
on her private parts,
who fondled her breasts
who stuck his penis in
until she started screaming,
but he said
he would tell her family
she was planning to run away
(she never told him
how did he know?)
so she was silent
and mute
and swore
she would never speak again
until she met me.

This is what I think
our people
we have it so bad
Ha Jia told me
there are now less rations
in the refugee camps;
he read it
in an article
one of the merchants gave to him.

This is what I know
this is a shitty world
(Ha Jia taught me this word)
where people do not have enough food to eat
where Zahura
is touched
by her brother's friend.

I will take care of you
you can sleep by my side
okay, I will not touch you
until you want me to
okay, if you never want me to touch you
I won't,
but I think you will, some time
never
okay
never.

It is nice
at night
to have someone sleep near me
I pretend
there is love in my world
like I once felt, Mama
when I had
a home.

Here
is her story
Zahura was in a camp
she could leave Myanmar
and the sweltering heat
of the camp
where her Mom and sister were
but she
had to marry a man
three times her age
and then she was promised Thailand
a home
a husband
like hundreds of thousands of girls.

This is what she knew:
she could read and write
and thought maybe
just maybe
she could be a doctor
since the teachers
in the hut
said she was smart,

and the man
had a mean look on his face
it was etched there
like a dent on a mountain.

Zahura said
the mothers, they are afraid
the alternative
to a husband
is a sale into sexual slavery.
Isn't this better?
her mother had asked her.

Better than what?

New York Times, 8/3/2015

She knew a girl
who also had dreams of working
in a hospital,
who now lives
in a suburb
of Kuala Lumpur
the Malaysian capital
caring for her mother
her ill sister
her sister's baby
in a cramped room
while waiting the return
of her husband
who disappeared
months ago
saying he was looking
for work.

New York Times, 8/3/2015

May-may,
don't tell me
the boys are getting thinner,
my sister is a stick.

Do you have any idea
what my life is like,
heavy water on my back
sweat like a set of skin,

but I have a girl
she sleeps far away from me,
soon
she will sleep close
so I can feel her breath,

and she will never leave me
maybe
I hope.

Let's count stars
she says,
and even though it is crazy
I do it
and it makes her giggle,
a tiny little thing
caught between my fingers
like a cricket.

You can make wishes
on a star,
she shares,
so I wish
to sleep closer to her,

only she tells me
not to tell her my wish
since then it will never,
ever
come true.

I lean over
and kiss her,
she doesn't stop me,
but she doesn't let it linger, either.
Next time.
Yes, next time.

The next day
Ha Jia asks me
if I am okay.

Why do you ask?

You are just acting different.

I tell him I am fine,

But what does it mean
to act different?

You hardly write
to May-may.

You need lots
of Kan-Kaung-ba-zay *

I have nothing
to tell,
but all I do is shrug my shoulders
as if to say
I do not know
what you are talking about.

*Good luck

Am I different because my body
is now covered with hair?

Am I different because
my clothes no longer fit,

I feel
as big as the tree.

Am I different because
I am so hungry
I would even eat a rat,

and I might,
since I need more meat.

I need meat.
I feel heat.

I must be fifteen
so much time
has passed. Your face is a blur
of forestry,

and *Pay-pay*,
you are dead
but I need to know
if this fire inside me,
sweltering summer heat fire
is normal.

You are sweet,
she says.

No I am not
I am angry
I could be a lizard
I could sneak up on you at night
I could eat you in one quick swallow.
I could kill
the mother who left me,
and leave all my siblings orphans.

I could kill you, too
because my body
is a tree
next to your branch.

But all I say is
thanks.

Why are you here?
You are too close.
Please, move away.

But I can't.
I want to feel her body
even for a moment;
I won't hurt her
just feel her breasts,
and I am so hungry for her.

She opens her mouth wide,
but she can't scream,
since she is hiding in these woods,

so I slip my tongue in her mouth,
but she bites me
breaks loose
runs away.

Stop.
Yaq!
Yaq!
I am sorry.

I say it louder
Stop, I am sorry
But I'm not.
Not really.

She runs
like the wind.
I am too tired
to run after her,

and angry
since all I really did
was kiss her.

I wouldn't have done anything else
unless she let me,

but she is like every woman
who runs away.

I had given her
half of my food for weeks
while I starved.

I lift my body,
but it won't move.

The night cries
and then it stops.
Cries
and then it stops.
It's not even
monsoon season.

Ha Jia calls me
a gentle giant,

but what about those ungentle feelings
what am I supposed to do
with them?

The night
is filled with ugly sounds,
and tonight
they are inside me:
growling
barking
scratching;

I may be the rat
that claws my way out of the dirt,
darting in and out of the woods
until I find her.

Phay loe ma thar *
I want to scream
and shout.

*Burmese profanity

She is lost
Zahura
I have looked everywhere,

sleep
never came
and now,

I must walk barefoot
because my sandals
no longer fit,

I am meant
to feel the splinters from the trees,

and carry
so much weight
on my broken back.

Water
pails and pails of water
I journey with water
on my back,

is it
a bucket of my tears
I carry back and forth
and to and from,

a bad burden.

This is what I know
as I lie on my back
and count the stars at night
(do you see stars, Mama?)

That each night
there is a different number

as if
they are disappearing
before my eyes,

and soon
there will be none.

And if
I saw her now
what would I do?

Stay away
like a leper
is that what she would want me to do?

Scream at her
so loud
the heavens might shake?

Or would I say
so
so sorry
for what I did
sorry that the world sucks

sorry I am a volcano
and I can't keep the lava
inside.

In my fantasy
I am a better person
not one who
figures women to be
rats on the run,

maybe, *May-may*
you made my heart hard
like slimy stone.

"What's wrong?"
"Nothing."
"Look at you–
Bags under your eyes
you drag your body
like a dead cow,
and you don't even eat
the little food I give you.
Do you want
to waste away?"

I want to tell Ha Jia
I am wasted
there is nothing left in me
if the rodents ate me for dinner tonight
I would be fine,

but all I do
is shrug.

She left me
and now there is nothing
for me to live for.

And then
I remember
I never told him
about Zahura,

and now I know
I have made it worse for her
If she ever comes back
(though she'll never come back),

She will be back
he says
this is what I know
she will be back.

How did you know?

I saw
the bounce in your step
the smile on your face
how sometimes you ate like a hog
other times
I had to force feed you
like a baby,

and you did not rip up your May-may's letters
not once
you may not have even read them.

I did not read them
well, sometimes I did.

Ha Jia
you can not tell anyone
she is already in trouble
she ran away
from an arranged marriage
at fourteen
she has already been raped.

I figured
he said,
edging closer to me
until he was so close
I could smell his smoke-stained breath,
until I cuddled in his arms
like a baby

and cried
and cried
and cried.

Oh, my son
my *boy, my boy*

he held me tight
like I was a boy
lost at sea
like a boat
rocking and rocking

and next thing I knew
for the first time in weeks
I was fast asleep
in his arms.

When I woke up
in his arms
there was a moment
when I saw the mountains
the forest
the blue skies
dreamed the sea
and I felt safe
like a smiling star,
just for
a still moment.

Gway htoot.
Gway htoot
Gway htoot *

Did you hear what I said
Gway-htoot
and *lee-gon*
and fuck.
I just learned this word
from one of these American teens
who came to visit Ha Jia
for whatever reason.

I hope you can hear me, *May-may*.
I hope you can, too,
Zahura.

*Burmese profanity

What are you saying?
Don't talk that way!!!
Those are nasty words!

What should I say?
My back is broken.
My heart is broken.
I will never see my family again.

What should I say?

You should say
everything will work out.

Bullshit.

I learned this word
too.

We will look for her
together
as soon as my nephew leaves,
there are just too many places to hide
in these woods,
and I know
all of them,
for I, too, had to hide
one time
for a very
long time.

I kiss him
and I hug him
and I tell him
I love him
though I am not sure
I love anyone.

I thought I loved Zahura
but she left me

like you did
and *Pay-pay*
and my sister
and my brothers.

There is no one left
to leave me.

Ha Jia
makes me read your last letter.

My dear Jubair,
not a day goes by
when I do not imagine you
what you look like
what you sound like,
what my tears would feel like
against your scratchy face;

yes, scratchy
since Ha Jia
tells me you are now
a man.

I never said *bhine*
to my boy,

and now he has turned
into a man.

How can I answer that
I do not feel
like a man;

I cry little boy tears
for my *May-may*
for my *Pay-pay*
for Zahura,

who perhaps I started to love
like a man.

But no one told me
how to treat a lady,
Pay-pay died
in silence,

and in our hut
we were swallowed
by silence,

too worried
about the next meal.

This is what I know
when you are worried
about where your next meal
is coming from,

that is all there is.

Now
I am ready
to learn
how to be a man
even though I am hungry
even though I am thirsty;

I want to know
how to touch a woman
without all the anger in my belly,
how to make her smile

how to give her all the trust
that I have lost
out at sea.

Wake up, son.

My sleep is a dead sleep.

Wake up, son.
It is time.
We will find her

I open my eyes
to the day
to Ha Jia's smiling
face
to his belief
in the impossible,

to his belief
in me
that he has called me son
that there are reapers in his hand
to cut through the forestry,

and for one
brief
moment in time
I believe
that the world
is filled with goodness.

But then I remember
Zahura is not just running from me
and my rage,

she is running
from the tsunami
of all the men
who have hurt her,

and she is good
at being a chameleon
she did it for a year
ate
and drank
from the little the woods
had to offer.

But I am ready
ready for discovery,
I will race with it
until I find it,

and though there are men
who want to destroy me and my people
and keep the women tame,

I will not let them
and Ha Jia will protect me.

I never heard sounds before
not like this,
it is a he
a mean man
who breathes heavily
and Ha Jia is small
so am I
these woods are laughing at us
ready
to bring us down.

Ha Jia tells me this story:
I ran away from home
I was young and stupid
and I did not want to be a farmer.
I dreamed I would find my way
to Bangkok,
and work for someone
so I could pay my way
to college.

I met your mother in these woods.
she had the same plans,
but I never touched her
because I was scared
she was so beautiful.

Why would that stop you?

Oh, she was more educated.
She talked of poetry
the light of the moon,
and how it would guide us
to a good place.

What made you come back?
What made May-may
return?

We were not going
anywhere
just woods
and more woods.
We stayed away
a long time.
Finally
we missed our families.

I miss my family
I am afraid
I will never see them again.

Ha Jia holds me
and we sleep
under the cover
of night
and the mean man
breathing heavily.

I am scared
of never seeing my family again
of never seeing Zahura
of the noises in the night
of the hunger in the day
(though Ha Jia has brought
nuts
and raisins
and berries);

I am scared
of being in this forest forever
oh, not the real forest,

the one with the brambles and branches
where there is no way out.

Ha Jia is amazing
he knows all these odd places to look
covered bush
dead leaves
dead trees,
and he has taught me
to crawl through this
so no one can hear
our footsteps;

tomorrow
we will travel at night,
better chance, maybe,
since she has to sleep
some time.

She has to sleep
some time in my heart.

She has to sleep
some time in my soul.

She has to sleep
so I can hear her breath.

She has to sleep
so I can smell her hair.

She has to sleep
so I can sleep, too,

since mostly
I am not sleeping.

Hard work
harder than the water pails,
crawling through bush,
sleeping
on dead limbs
of trees,
bathing in dirty streams,
just so she won't smell the sweat of men
which Ha Jia says
is easy to smell,

and walking
walking
walking
with no direction.

We crawl through the night
on our hands and knees.

We crawl through the night
and I am told
to not breathe so heavily,
to keep my coughs silent.

We crawl through the night
where I never knew
so many small animals
crawling up my arms and legs,

and then
and then
and then
there she is
sleeping
hidden in a tree.

I want to scream.
I want to shout.
I want to jump up and down.

Shh
Ha Jia tells me.
Do not awaken her
she will be scared
she will try to run
and will get hurt.

We will block
her exit from this tree
and sleep in front of it,
and when she awakens
we will be there.

Oh,
she looks
no older
than a young child.

Sleep, son.
Sleep.

No.
No.
No.

Fear.
Terror.

It is fine.
You are safe.
We will take care of you.

It is fine.
You are safe.
We will take care of you.

Ha Jia says this
over and over.
And suddenly
words, which I usually love
have all but disappeared.

Tell her,
son;
tell her
how you feel.

I am so
so
so
so
so
so
so
so sorry.

I will never
ever
never
ever
never hurt you again.

And I will never leave you,
I add,

but she looks at me
with those large, dark eyes
and I can tell
she does not know
whether to run–
or not,

but when Ha Jia says
come back with us, Zahura,

she falls into my arms
and cries
cries
cries
like all the tears in the world
are inside of her.

Cha-ma-chin-go-chit-the *
I tell her.

Cha-nor-kin-mya-go chit-teh,
she tells me back.

* I love you!

We walk back together
I hold her hand
and Ha Jia
assures her
that her secret
is safe with us,

and I promise
never again to touch her
unless she wants to
and her eyes tell me
she does.

We hold hands
as we walk,
and Ha Jia
sings a song
with the woods,
about the trees
how they will protect us,
and keep us from harm.

I missed you
I could not l sleep without you,

I missed you, too
I dreamed about you
every night.

I am sorry.
I am so, so sorry.
I say it again
because of her silence.

I know
she says
I wanted you to find me.

So why did you run away?

You scared me
I have known
too many violent men;
vicious boys
become violent men.

Everyone always told me
I was sweet
I never knew
I had that in me.

Sorry.
Sorry.
Sorry.

I fantasize
you say that to me
instead of the bullshit letters
where you tell me
how little you had for lunch.
Bullshit.

Whoever taught me
to say sorry?

Surely not
YOU.

We walk.
I hold her hand
like a leaf
I will protect
from storms.

Walk
till the bottom of my feet
are the forest
filled with mud and muck,
and the splinters
bite me,
they bite Zahura, too,
who I want to carry,
but I can't,

and finally
we arrive
back home.

Is this our home?
the forest of nowhere.

Now what?
I look to Ha Jia
for answers.

Now you will get back to work
and the two of you
will get back to learning
you will read
and write
both of you.

And at night
when the sky goes to sleep
you, my son,
will protect her.

You will sleep close
and tight,
and speak to no one
about this
not even my wife
or children.

I understand
how hard this must be
for Ha Jia
who went with me
for days,
whose feet
have bigger blisters to bear,

and now must make up
some excuse
to his family
of where he went,

and then he shows me
the fish he has caught
in the stream.

I have gone fishing
for food,

the sun shines through
the missing teeth
in his smile.

How do I know
he won't rat me out?

How do I know
I can trust him?

Do you understand
if they find me
they will kill me,
do you understand that?

How do I know
I can trust you?

I put my arms around her
and steer her close to me.

This is what I know:
Ha Jia can be trusted
I trust him
more than myself.

That night
our bodies are wrapped around
the other
like we own
the same skin;

you can't tell
where her small arm begins
and my large one
ends,

and for the first time
in a long time
I sleep,
way after the sun has come up,

and Ha Jia
is smiling like a lunatic
when I come
to fetch my pails
at noon.

Min-ga-la-ba *
she says.

Can I help you?
I feel so useless,

Here
read this.

I give her
The Good Earth
the book I told you about
the one by Pearl S. Buck,

and she reads like she is ravenous,
and by the afternoon, after I have fetched many
pails of water

she asks for more
more.
More!

*Good morning

I think she means books
(which she does),
but she also means
me,
the kiss
I just gave her.
She doesn't want to let go
like we are on raft
and know we won't drown
since we have each other.

What are you doing?
She turns to me
in the middle of the night.

What does it look
like I am doing?

Smoking a cigarette
Why?
Are you an idiot?
Nga lo chit mae thu *

When you were gone
I was lonely,
and I wanted
to be a man,

so I saved them
found them
in town,
and I smoked them;
they were
my friends.

Idiot, she says.

*You are driving me crazy

I am crying
I can't stop it
I never did this
in front of her,
and the
mosquitoes
can't shut up.

She takes
the cigarette
out of my mouth,
(makes certain the light is out)
moves my arms to my side
rubs them up and down
like I am an infant,
drags me down
to the ground
takes me
a man
double her size
into her lap

where she rocks me
sings to me
says
she will protect me.

In the middle
of that dank and dreary night
my face still moist
my breath still saturated
with smoke,

I find her
on top of me;
her tongue
slips effortlessly
into my mouth,

and we are rocking
our ripped clothes
tossed wildly to the side.

I trust you
she says,

and that night
sleep is a dream
of happiness,

and when morning comes to greet us
we are the ones
who have set the sun
on fire.

The mosquitoes
feel less itchy
the smell
of dead dogs
does not bother me
since I smell
her hair,

the trees
applaud her
with the little air
the earth has given them.

And this
becomes our routine
each night,

and I am never tired
no matter how many pails of water
I must carry.

Sometimes
Zahura helps me.
Other times
she rests beneath the umbrella
of the tree
reading,
telling me
she is plotting our escape.

Suddenly
the brazen bugs
seem beautiful.

Part III: The Great Escape

I believe
we can escape
like we do at night
inside each other,
legs wrapped around
each other,
arms entwined
like branches
my breath
to her breath,

so mosquitoes
monkeys
dead dogs
water rats
leave us
to our dreams.

You have to read this
I do not know what it says
your Mama wrote Private
and Important
on the envelope.

Now,
Ha Jia demands
and not in front of Zahura.
You have to honor
your mother's request.

Why?

Because that is the law
of the land.

Ha!
what law
what land
when you are invisible?

Jubair,

You must not tell Ha Jia.
You must not tell anyone.
Talking may mean
risking the lives of the ones
you love.

You cannot say good-bye
not to anyone.
This is dangerous
what you are about to do.

In three days
on Friday
you are to go
to the woods a mile behind Ha Jia's house
where you fetch the water
at dawn.
A woman
will be waiting for you.
She is a Mama
like me,
so no one will suspect her;

she knows where to take you
what boat you are to go on,

where you will travel
to Thailand,

where we will meet you
with open arms
when you get
here.

PS No one.
Not even
the monkeys in the forest
do you understand?

You risk the lives
of anyone you tell,

I have already registered you
for a school
they have set up
at the camps.

NOOOOOOOOOOOOOOOOOOOOOOO!!!!!!!!!!!!!!!
I wail,

knowing
I am so far away,
no one
can hear me
curse these wet and wild woods
curse they day I was born

curse my mother
for tempting me
to leave the one
I love.

I cannot.
I will not.
I cannot.
I will not.
I will stay here
with Zahura,
until I die.
Until we both die
together
since there is no food
no job
no place for us
to continue
to survive.

May-may
how could you do this to me?

I cry to the Gods
I cry to the pagoda
on my arm.
I cry to my dead *Pay-pay*
I cry to Ha Jia
for not taking us into
his home.

If I take Zahura
we will both die.
If I go
only she dies.

But I love her
yet I know
I have to go.

Three days
and I cannot say
good-bye.

I will live and get smarter with books,
but inside I will be a dead tree.

What's wrong?

Nothing.

Liar.
last night
you tossed and turned
and cried out in your sleep
for the gods to forgive you.

The gods
will never forgive me.
I will never
forgive myself.

Stop being crazy!

I was so inhuman to you.

That was in the past.

No
I want to say
it is only beginning
and I have to have faith.
Ha Jia, who is more of a man than I am,
will figure things out
and take care of her,

165

maybe figure out a way
of sending her
to me.

Are you turning lazy on me
Jubair?

No. Sorry, Ha Jia.
I am just tired
so, so tired.

Take a day off.

Oh no,
I can't.

Because I am leaving
the day after tomorrow.
Please take care of her.
Please bring her
into your home,
please read my mind,

if I do not get educated
there is nothing I can do
to save anyone.

You know I love you
I tell him.

No matter where you go
or what you do

I know you love me
so do not worry yourself.

I cry
and for the last time
forever
I am cradled
in his arms.

You are acting
like a mae thu person *
tell me what is wrong.

It is just
I love you
so much,
I am afraid.

Will you love me
no matter
what?

Of course
you crazy, crazy boy,

no matter what.

If only you know
tomorrow when you wake up
I will not be here.

I am with you
forever,
no matter what.

*Crazy

169

The drums
of the night
are going crazy:

the yelping of dogs
the hissing of snakes
the rage of mosquitoes
and dying dogs,

and I am being dragged
through all of this
by this woman
no more than ninety pounds-
my mother's friend.

You are too slow
do you want to
get caught?
she hisses,

yes
I want to be dragged through
the sewers of Bangkok.
Can't you smell my stench?

No.
Though my heart feels
different.

Zahura
I know you hate me.
You will hate me forever
the way I hated my *May-may*
for a long, long time.

I wanted to say *bhine*.
I really did,
but that would have hurt you
even more.

Truly
Cha-ma-chine-go-chit-the.
Forever.

For real?
I am not going
in that boat.
It is not much longer
than my leg
and look, dozens of people
are lined up.
Doesn't the trip take hours?

You are going.
Are you kidding me?
You know how much your Mama paid
to take you?
Do you know what I risked
to take you here?

Risk.
That is what Zahura did
not you
lady.

In a week's time
you must give these letters
to Ha Jia.

Are you kidding me?
she asks.

If I ever see
land again
he will be safe
and I will be safe
on land
and he must know to take care
of my girl.

She laughs,
but the way she rubs my hand
and gazes into my eyes
I feel she will do
the right thing.

Ha Jia,

I had to leave,
but I can share nothing with you
other than
my urgent plea:

please care for my Zahura
like she is one of yours
tell her that I love her
tell her that I had no choice
tell her I am not
a slimy snake,

but a boy with
too many tears
inside.

After you read this letter
burn it,
but the other one
please hide
until it is safe
to hand it over
to Zahura.

Many people weep
the man
who is sending his older children
alone,

and they are crying
for *May-may*,
but there is no *May-may*;

there are mothers
holding their children, too many,
bony and bawling babies,

and a few old people, too
who look like they have
no skin on them.

We are all traveling
on this desperate boat
to nowhere,

and this is what I left
Zahura for.

All I have brought
on this journey
is one book,
The Good Earth,
the clothes on my back
the letters you wrote
the sorrow that sits in me
that fills me up
from head to toe.

What is Ha Jia
thinking now?

So many people
carry nothing
but their bodies.

The sea is vile;
it is violent
it rocks the dozens of us
trapped
in this casket of cargo
back and forth
like we are the dead dogs
in the water,

so many people throw up
and scream,
but I don't do anything like that;

I gaze
at the sickly sky,
wondering
if there is a god
how could he possibly
leave us to the mercy
of a random ocean
and smugglers,
who pass around bread,

as if that is enough
for all this hunger.

I have lost track
of the waves
of time
and water,
so much water,

yet still I sweat,
heat is a shroud
that hangs over us
taunting us
to stay alive
with no
compelling reason.
I decide to read
May-may's first letter.

Why I Did not Say *Bhine*

By now
you must hate me.
You are hearing this
in Ha Jia's voice
since you can not
read or write yet,
but you will
I assure you,
I know
because you are the child
I could leave behind.

How could any mother
leave any child behind?
I really don't know,
but I am certain
the months ahead
will be torture.

Jubair,
God gave me no choice.
I know you do not believe in God,
but I would like to believe
there is someone out there
who will make things better
one day.

Our lives in Myanmar
were dreadful
I think you know this,
and this is what I knew
I had to get the family
out of there
anywhere;
I heard Thailand would be better.
We shall see.
I saved for this ocean journey
for years.
I never thought
ever
I could not take my whole family
with me,

but the smugglers
they increase the price per body.
Can you imagine,
they make you pay
per body?
Your sister,
still on my breast,
was the same price
as your big brother.

So why
were you

the child left behind?
my smack-in-the-middle child
between two boys,
one big and boastful,
but filled with fluff,
the other small and scared
of his own shadow,

and then there was you,
Jubair
brave
brilliant
strong
resilient;

you
my special son
who I had faith
would learn
to read and write
would survive
the storms
and sleeping in the woods,
the one who could make it.

And I never said good-bye
because I knew
I would see you once again.

There
in the middle of a monsoon
the boat tossing and turning
like a crazy person,

but straight ahead
there is a dock
and I can see
my sister,
my brothers
bigger
better
smiling,
oblivious to the rain,

and behind them
my mother
my father
(who I knew had never died)
and a whole
new
world
waiting
to say hello.

Dear Zahura,

I had to leave,
but this is what I know

I did not need
to say *bhine*
because I will find a way
to come back to you.

I hand my note
to the captain of the ship
(that is what he calls himself)
the one I read to
through days and nights
of storms
and smelly bodies.
He likes me.
I know he will get this letter to you.
I will return.
Sooner
not later.

The Illustrator

Dr. Bashar Ericsoossi is originally from Syria. He is board-certified in Nephrology and Internal Medicine. In 2007, he received his medical degree from Damascus University School of Medicine in Syria. When not practicing medicine in New York City, Dr Ericsoossi sees the world through the eyes of art. Since childhood, he has been expressing himself through art that echoes both his thoughts and his emotions.

The Author

Pamela L. Laskin is a lecturer in the English Department at City College, where she directs the Poetry Outreach Center. Her book *Ronit and Jamil*, A Palestinian/Israeli *Romeo and Juliet* in verse, published by Harper Collins in 2017, was one of *School Library Journal's* 17 2017 YA Books To Have On Your Radar, one of *Entertainment Weekly's* 34 Most Anticipated Novels of 2017, and was a 2018 Sydney Taylor notable book. *BEA*, a picture book, was a finalist for the Katherine Paterson Prize for Children's Fiction. Pamela is the winner of the 2018 Leapfrog Fiction contest for YA fiction. She teaches graduate and undergraduate children's writing. Follow her on twitter at twitter@RonitandJamil, and follow her blog at http://PamelaLaskin.blogspot.com/.